THE FAIRY DOGMOTHER

Caroline Crowe   Richard Merritt

LITTLE TIGER

LONDON

It was a perfectly ordinary day at Woofington's Dog Shelter. Cinders had helped Bernard dig for dinosaurs, given Boots some mountain climbing tips and was just wondering what was for lunch, when . . .

To Ellie, wagracadabra!
And thank you ~ C C

For Erin ~ R M

LITTLE TIGER PRESS LTD,
an imprint of the Little Tiger Group
1 Coda Studios, 189 Munster Road, London SW6 6AW
Imported into the EEA by Penguin Random House Ireland,
Morrison Chambers, 32 Nassau Street, Dublin D02 YH68
www.littletiger.co.uk

First published in Great Britain 2021
Text copyright © Caroline Crowe 2021
Illustrations copyright © Richard Merritt 2021
Caroline Crowe and Richard Merritt have asserted their rights
to be identified as the author and illustrator of this work
under the Copyright, Designs and Patents Act, 1988
A CIP catalogue record for this book is available
from the British Library

All rights reserved · ISBN 978-1-80104-000-6
Printed in China · LTP/2800/3735/0321
2 4 6 8 10 9 7 5 3 1

WAGRACADABRA!

"Priscilla Paws," coughed a voice.
"Fairy dogmother, at your service."

Cinders was understandably
surprised. "Fairy DOGmother?"
he woofed.

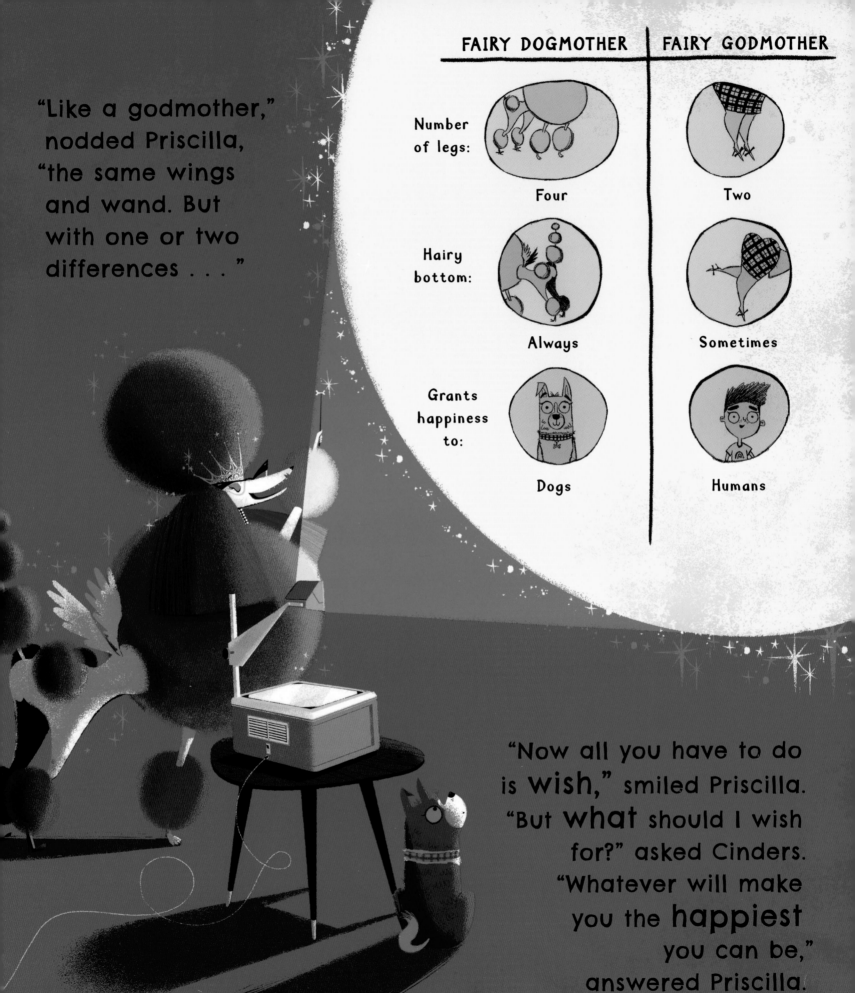

"Like a godmother," nodded Priscilla, "the same wings and wand. But with one or two differences . . ."

FAIRY DOGMOTHER	FAIRY GODMOTHER
Number of legs: Four	Two
Hairy bottom: Always	Sometimes
Grants happiness to: Dogs	Humans

"Now all you have to do is **wish**," smiled Priscilla. "But **what** should I wish for?" asked Cinders. "Whatever will make you the **happiest** you can be," answered Priscilla.

But Cinders was already pretty happy.
    "I have a cosy bed and food to eat.
Lots of friends and holes to dig,"
he told Priscilla.

"I hate to hurry you,"
interrupted Priscilla,
"but wishes have a time
limit! Chop, chop!
This clock won't
stop."

"It's no good!"
said Cinders, rolling onto
his back. "I'm stuck."
So Cinders did what he
always did when
he had a problem.

He asked his friends for help.
Of course **everyone** had
a suggestion.

"I know what I'd wish for!" barked Ruff and Tuff together. **"Sausages!"**

"True happiness is a **bone!"** suggested Titch.

"Wouldn't you like, just for once, to catch your **tail?"** asked Gruff.

Priscilla shook her head.
"I wouldn't recommend it . . ."

"But lickety-split," she added.
"The clock is ticking."
And it really was, **loudly**,
which was quite distracting.

"I'd love **longer legs**,"
sighed Pebbles.

"Imagine the possibilities!" chorused Bernard, Boots and Tallulah.

"I'd wish for a ball!" shouted Boris.

"A wonderful idea!"
Priscilla winked.

"I know he didn't
mean that kind of ball, but
fairy godmothers aren't the only
ones who love to dance!"

Soon wishes were coming
so fast that Cinders couldn't
keep track.

"I wish I could climb trees!"

"I want to waterski!"

"To ride a unicycle!"

"To go into space!"

"To be a cat!"

And time was nearly up!

10, 9, 8, 7 . . .

"It's no good," cried Cinders.
"I can't pick!"

Then Old Wally, from the
end of the row, barked,
"What about a real owner?"

And everyone went quiet.

Because the one thing they wanted –
more than anything –
was someone to love them
and take them home.

Suddenly Cinders knew
exactly what to do . . .

"I wish for all my friends to find perfect homes with people who love them," he smiled.
And with a flick of Priscilla's wand, they did.

Cinders' tail was the waggiest of all. His friends were the happiest they could be and it was all because of him.

"Thanks, Cinders!" woofed Pebbles. "You're the BEST!"

It was a bit quiet when everyone had gone.
At least Priscilla hadn't left yet.
    "Thank you for my wish," Cinders said. "Do you think maybe they'll come back for visits?"

    "In my experience,"
smiled Priscilla, "fairy tails
always have a happy ending."

And she was right. Because across town, Alf had just asked his fairy godmother for . . .

"A best friend!"

And that's how
Alf met Cinders.

Because as you know . . .

. . . Cinders is absolutely the very best friend anyone could wish for. Just ask them!